Following The FOLLOWERS

Guru Kripa Deep Singh

FanatiXx Publication

FanatiXx® Publication

Rourkela | Mumbai | Delhi NCR | Ahmedabad

Following The Followers
By Guru Kripa Deep Singh

ISBN: **978-93-7406-015-5**

First Edition – 2025

This is an Original Work of the Author.
All works of the author's imagination.
Any resemblance to actual persons, living or dead, is purely coincidental.

For permissions, inquiries, or feedback:
Email: outreach@fanatixx.info
Instagram: @fanatixxpublication

About the Author:

Guru Kripa Deep Singh is a poet, filmmaker, content creator, and truth-seeker born in 2002 in Delhi. Raised in a middle-class family, with dogs as his earliest companions, his formative years were marked by struggle, resilience, and observation. Thankful to those who stood by him in difficult times, he chose distance learning over a toxic academic environment while building a digital presence through creative reels that reached millions. Learning continuously from nature and society, his work reflects a deep critique of greed, blindness, and human complacency. Following the Followers, his debut novelette, transforms India's sacred scars into a literary exploration of truth and humanity

Email: gurukripadeepsinghbhasin13@gmail.com
Instagram: @guru_kripa13

Summary for Following the Followers:

In a smog-choked Delhi, where truth is sold as relics and gods are caged in code, the Curious Man dares to scream. Following the Followers traces his quest, abandoning property, family, and past for enlightenment's unadorned heart. Haunted by his sister's ghost, wielding a camera and journal, he exposes Acharya Rudra's empire of commodified faith. From Bodh Gaya's golden idols to Amritsar's langar, his path winds through India's sacred wounds. But truth is a wound that sings, and his scream sparks a mob's worship and wrath, tearing him apart like vultures. A boy and a girl clutch his relics—t-shirt, journal, camera—following the followers, blind to the humanity he died for. Guru Kripa Deep Singh's poetic, brutal masterpiece shatters faith, ethics, and sanity, a Nietzschean cry against greed that dares readers to face the truth they kill, fearing its unbearable weight.

Synopsis for Following the Followers:

In a Delhi choked by smog and greed, where truth is peddled as relics and gods are caged in digital streams, the Curious Man abandons wealth, family, identity—everything—for the unadorned heart of enlightenment. Following the Followers, a searing literary odyssey by Guru Kripa Deep Singh, traces his quest through India's sacred and broken paths, haunted by his sister's ghost, a whisper from her hospital bed: "Truth feeds the hungry." With a camera that captures lies and a journal bleeding ink, he seeks humanity's pulse, not rituals or babas, only to confront Acharya Rudra's empire—a glittering syndicate selling faith through apps, QR codes, and relic auctions.

The Curious Man's journey winds through Bodh Gaya, where golden idols mock a luminary's truth, and Sarnath, where QR-coded prayers turn silence into commerce. Kushinagar's burning corpses and Amritsar's langar, pulsing with equality, stir his heart, while Dharamsala's poisoned peaks and a Sufi shrine's cracked dome, where he finds Sarmad's coin, sear his soul with authenticity's weight. Each step strips him raw, his sister's ghost heavier than his fraying journal, his camera a noose of light exposing commodified lies. Delhi's heart, a beast of steel and smog, becomes his battleground as he infiltrates Rudra's ashram and market, uncovering a server hub that cages truth in code.

His scream—a viral exposé of Rudra's fraud—splits the city. Half worship him as a savior, half brand him a traitor. Rudra's enforcers hunt him through alleys and temples, vials of poison glinting. In a public square, the Curious Man confronts Rudra, camera raised, voice jagged as lightning: "Truth is no relic—it's a wound that sings!" But the mob, a sea of phones and fists, turns on him. A boy clutches his t-shirt, a girl his journal's torn page, as they tear him apart—vultures in human skin. Poison burns his veins, his sister's whisper fading, Sarmad's coin hot as his ebbing blood. He forgives them—"They know not what they tear"—but his truth is buried, his body left without a grave, relics scattered to Rudra's market.

Silence screams louder than death. The boy's eyes, dry as stone, and the girl's trembling tears reflect a world that worships scraps, not truth. Rudra's screens flash the Curious Man's face, selling his death as salvation. A man chants "Baba," another spits "Traitor," following the followers, blind to the humanity he died for. The journal's ashes scatter, its final words—"Truth is a wound that sings, eternal, clean as water, wild as fire, fierce as lightning"—unheard. The Curious Man's ghostly echo laments: his death was no whale's fall feeding the hungry, but a waste, slain by the human beast that crowns its truth-bearers only to tear them apart. He sees what the great ones saw: humanity, the highest mind, is the fool that kills its own light, worshipping relics over enlightenment.

Yet a spark flickers in the unseen—a boy, a girl, carrying his wound in their bones, a revolution unborn. Guru Kripa Deep Singh's Following the Followers is a poetic, brutal cry against greed, a Nietzschean wound that shatters faith, ethics, and sanity. Through India's sacred scars, it exposes the human beast's claws, sharper than any vulture's, taught by none but itself. The Curious Man's truth, buried by those following the followers, sings for the hungry, the free, daring readers to face the unbearable: "Truth is dead, and we have killed it." —Guru Kripa Deep Singh.

Acknowledgments

Following the Followers is a wound carved from my journey's scars — truths and struggles survived, lessons sharper than love lost.

I bow to my mother, whose hands fed dogs, birds, and cows, weaving compassion into my soul. To my father, Shri Dr. S. Taranjeet Singh Bhasin, blind yet clear in truth, who steadied me through every fall. To my first friends — dogs — whose selfless seva outshone human bonds.

I honor the late Shri Baba Girja Shankar Ji, my guardian angel, who loved me as his own and whose memory still feeds my fire.

With eternal gratitude, I remember the late Kailash Devi, who embraced me as her grandchild when bloodlines said I was not. Her love was so boundless it bent rituals and traditions, allowing me to walk beside her family in her final rites. Though she is not here to hold this book in her hands, her name will live within its pages as it lives in me.

To family and friends, whose love eclipsed struggle. To Shri Guru Gobind Singh Sahib Ji, whose sacrifices for humanity light this cry against greed. I am proud to be your Sikh, your son.

—Guru Kripa Deep Singh

Writer's Note

Following the Followers is a wound born from my scars—rescuing animals who couldn't be saved, their silent hearts heavier than the universe in my hands. A lovebird, meant for a neighbor's child, died in a day; three dogs from my street, poisoned, fell without knowing betrayal or envy. Burying them with bare hands, I felt the weight of angels—God's first children, whose seva is supreme.

Yet Rumi whispered: "Bury a seed, a tree grows; death is a gate to the true Creator, the sun falling here but rising there."

This novelette is lit by my mother's compassion, the love of the late Shri Baba Girja Shankar Ji, the truth of my father, Shri Dr. S. Taranjeet Singh Bhasin, blind yet piercing, and the memory of the late Kailash Devi, who embraced me as her own grandchild beyond the bounds of blood. To Shri Guru Gobind Singh Sahib Ji, whose sacrifices for humanity burn like an eternal flame, I bow in reverence.

The Curious Man's truth, like those angels, sings for the unseen—will you hear it?

—Guru Kripa Deep Singh

Contents

Epigraph

The world is a safari for the rich—
from air-conditioned jeeps they watch us burn,
call our screams tradition, our blood holy.

We follow the followers—
not the light, but its shadow in silk robes;
not the truth, but those who sell it in temples and markets.

In greed's safari, elites cage truth in gilded lies,
while mobs chant blind in Rudra's screens.
But God lives in the hungry belly,
in the broken spine of a street dog,
in hands feeding the voiceless without filming for fame.
You won't find nirvana in incense or mantras,
but in silent seva—
a wound daring you to look.
This is not a story.
It's a wound.
Bleeding until someone dares to feel.
—Guru Kripa Deep Singh

Dedication

To the ceaseless storm in my mind, Guru Kripa Deep Singh, where overthinking weaves its tangled roots—this dedication takes shape. To this society, a fractured glass reflecting rituals that bind us in silent chains, and the cruelty we etch with trembling hands. To ignorance, a shroud over our souls, and the shadowed corridors of mental health where echoes of despair linger. To loneliness, a shadow that walks beside me, and the fleeting peace we grasp amid struggle's jagged edges. To diseases that gnaw at our bones, to aging that paints time's relentless decay, and to death—the quiet unraveling, as Buddha glimpsed in the frail stoop, the anguished groan, the final hush.

This is for the animals too, their tongues chanting the universe's unspoken hymns—lions roaring primal truths, vultures tracing wisdom in silent spirals. They speak in a language of flesh and instinct, beyond our words, yet we stumble, deaf to their song. This is also for every messiah who walked upon this earth—Nanak, Buddha, and all who bore the light—whose footsteps echo through time, guiding us through the mire. This book, a pilgrimage through life's dark marrow and back, is forged from my own restless spirit. To the human in me, scarred and seeking, and to you, reader, who bears the same weight—10 out of infinity, a humble mark on the boundless canvas we strive to comprehend.

Chapter 1:

Tracks to Truth Prologue

The train shuddered and growled as it left Patna Junction, iron wheels gnawing at steel tracks like hungry beasts. I pressed my palm to the cold glass, watching the city's neon promises dissolve into dust-choked fields. Straw huts crouched at the horizon, skull-white under the late-afternoon sun. A billboard intruded on the view: ENLIGHTENMENT NOW AVAILABLE – CALL FOR DETAILS. I swallowed a laugh. I knew better than any slogan.

I'd carved out a name for myself in the wild—Nat Geo, BBC—my camera a passport to nature's most brutal theaters. Lions tearing flesh, vultures igniting the sky with their circling wings, an elephant calf's last gasp before death. I'd endured scorching deserts and monsoon torrents, climbed cliffs slick with rain, and stood in frozen forests where breath crystallized in midair. I'd seen life and death at their rawest, unvarnished.

And still, I was running from a question: What is the point of all this?

As I aged, the lens grew heavy not just with glass but with doubt. I'd watched humans with keener interest than beasts—counting coins in hospital corridors, eyes dim behind brand-name frames; lovers promising forever while clutching smartphones; monks hawking retreats online. I'd witnessed more diseases than cures, invisible ailments that corroded minds. I'd seen money worshipped as deity and discarded as worthless paper. I'd watched friendships forged and shattered like glass; betrayals cloaked in polite smiles.

Why do we pretend none of it matters?

I tightened my grip on the camera strap. Its leather was soft from years of use—my only honest companion. I opened my notebook and spread my backstory across the page:

I was successful in my field; my career had its ups and downs.
I captured shots no one had ever seen—wild buffalo charging monsoon floods, snow-leopards slipping between rocks, the last moments of a dying antelope.

I observed humans closely, knowing I too would leave this world—and wondering what, if anything, I'd leave behind.

I felt lost: a lifetime of questions, yet no map. So one day I walked away—no goodbyes—ensuring those who depended on me were safe, then vanished into the raw core of life.

The carriage lights flickered; for a heartbeat, darkness reigned. In that flash, I saw every certainty bleed away.

Enlightenment is that blackout—when you realize everything you trusted is an illusion.

When the glow returned, a vendor hovered with samosas and bottled water. I shook my head. He moved on, eyes searching for the next buyer. Like vultures I'd filmed, humans honed in on weakness—one tremor, one crack—and descended with polite brutality.

Suddenly, a commotion erupted near the door. A transgender woman, sari faded and eyes burning with desperation, confronted a young man who'd refused to pay her for blessings. "No money? But you have this gift!" she spat, grabbing him low, her fingers closing on his testicles. His scream cut through the carriage; passengers recoiled into silence. She hissed, "God gave you these—offer them now, or I'll place a baddua upon you!" The man stumbled back, shock and humiliation in his eyes, while the vendor wove through the crowd as if nothing had happened. Harassment in the name of god—just raw greed and fear cloaked in superstition.

I climbed into the aisle. At a deserted platform, a lone monk sat cross-legged on cracked concrete, saffron robes stained by dust and meditation. He exhaled slowly; the world fell away. His calm was an accusation.

"Bodh Gaya?" I asked, voice brittle against the engine's roar.

He opened his eyes—dark pools reflecting every bit of my restless soul—and merely nodded.

My thoughts bled into one another:

What is darkness? The absence of light—or the moment you confront your own shadow?
What is enlightenment? A flash of insight—or the long, cold burn of truth?
What is time? A prison we build with moments we fear to lose.
What is death? A shutter click closing the frame—or the silence that outlives breath?
What is intelligence? Mastery of abstract laws—or scars carved by honesty?

I remembered questions I'd carried: Why are babies fearless until someone teaches them to be afraid? Can an illiterate heart be wiser than learned minds? If I ruled the world, would I taste life's bitter edge—or drown in comfort's lull? Should I pray to gods we invented, or give my donations to demons, beggars, or perhaps no one at all? Should I embrace my inner child or force myself to grow up?

A whistle cut through my reverie. Dawn was bleeding across the sky in bruised purples and reds, as if the world itself had been wounded. I slung my pack over one shoulder—gear and questions both heavy against my spine.

The doors slid open. I stepped onto the platform, humid air clawing at my lungs. Somewhere ahead stood the Bodhi Tree—ancient, unyielding, silent witness to the fall and rise of every soul.

I tightened my camera strap, not as armor, but as a promise: I will look without flinching. I will strip away every illusion.

Here begins the real journey—into life's heart of darkness and back again.

Chapter 2:

Under the Bodhi Tree

I stepped off the train into Bodh Gaya's humid choke, incense clawing my lungs. Dawn bled through the Mahabodhi Temple's spires, staining the stones blood-red and gold. My camera bag sagged—heavy with lenses and every question I'd scrawled since Patna's neon lies faded behind me.

I'd chased the wild's brutal truth for years—Nat Geo, BBC. Lionesses ripping flesh at dusk, vultures tearing at still-warm carcasses, herds crumbling to plague. Blood never shook me. One rule held: don't interfere. Nature grinds on; I just watched. But the lens got heavier with age, doubt piling up like dust. My sister's death cracked me open—her dog-eared book on Buddha, left on her hospital bed, burned in my mind. She'd read of a prince who ditched everything—palace, wife, son—to face life's rot. I felt that itch too, that need to strip away the lies. He saw an old man's stoop, a sick man's groan, a corpse's stillness. It woke him. I needed what he found.

The courtyard was a mess of crushed petals, ground into stone by pilgrims' feet. Incense coiled around gilded Buddhas, their shine mocking the decay they hid. My boots scraped ancient flagstones, expecting silence. Instead, chants clashed with scooter drones and distant horns.

A monk slid from a gleaming SUV, robes crisp, thumb scrolling a smartphone. He glanced up, blinked, then scrolled on. Not the barefoot ascetic I'd imagined—more like the billboard from Patna promising "ENLIGHTENMENT NOW AVAILABLE." A whisper in the crowd mentioned Swami Dhanraj, some big-shot guru who'd blessed this monk's ride. My stomach churned.

An old guide hobbled over, staff tapping stone, eyes glinting with mischief. "First time, beta?" he asked in Hindi.

"Yeah. Tell me about him."

He pointed to the Bodhi Tree's gnarled branches, older than time. "Siddhartha Gautama. Prince. Ditched his palace, wife, son. Saw age, sickness, death—ran straight for truth. Sat there, fought his demons, found nirvana. Freedom from this muck."

I nodded, seeing my own restlessness in that story. But his face darkened, voice dropping. "When he died, they tore him apart like hyenas. Sanchi got his ashes, Sri Lanka his tooth. They carved up his body to clutch at power."

My gut twisted. "After he said let it all go?"

He spat into the dust. "They needed something to hold. Built statues he'd hate, piled offerings at their feet." He nodded at a golden Buddha, dripping with coins. "Some even say the Dalai Lama carries his soul."

"His soul?" I pressed. "If he hit nirvana, why come back?"

His grin was sharp. "Maybe to guide. Maybe he's gone. Who knows?"

A roar shattered the moment—pilgrims clawing at a fallen Bodhi leaf. Hands ripped like jackals over carrion, nails scraping bark, voices snarling, petals pulped under frantic feet. Blood welled on a woman's wrist; she didn't stop. I'd filmed beasts fighting for scraps, but this was worse—humans shredding a leaf that brushed his shadow.

I slipped into the tree's shade, its quiet swallowing the chaos. Buddha stared down life's filth—disease, death, decay—and mastered it. So why did his followers claw at bones, kneel to gold, chase leaves? He ditched riches; they drowned in comfort. He hunted truth; they split it into Theravāda's rules,

Mahāyāna's spirits, Vajrayāna's shadows. His words twisted in their hands, like my sister's book, now just a memory in a world chasing hashtags.

I closed my eyes, jungle and temple merging in my skull. I didn't want their mess. I wanted his clarity.

Tomorrow, I'd sit where he sat, legs crossed, back to the tree.

Tonight, I'd watch—let the darkness show me what the light buried.

Chapter 3:

The Weight of Stillness

I returned to the Bodhi Tree at dusk. The sky was bruised purple, and a heavy hush settled over the courtyard—an almost holy silence, or the calm before a storm. I chose a low, weathered stone slab, its surface cracked by ancient roots and human devotion. I dropped my camera bag beside it and sat down, legs folding against rigid limbs and a spine that protested with every shift.

The air was thick with humidity and the scent of incense that curled around me like smoke through broken ruins. My shirt clung to my back; sweat slid down my neck in cold rivulets. I closed my eyes, breathing in the damp earth, the distant hum of cicadas, the soft clink of temple bells. In the wild, I learned that stillness was death's whisper—predators watched without blinking. Here, I was the prey of my own mind.

Thoughts erupted: the lioness's jaws clamped around bone; the hospital ward's neon glare; the leaf-fight beneath these very branches. My chest heaved as doubt roared: What is stillness if my mind never stops bleeding questions? Every inhale felt like pulling razor wire through my lungs; every exhale, a surrender I couldn't stomach.

I forced my back straight, recalling the guide's words: "Freedom from the muck." But muck clung to me—memories, regrets, the weight of a thousand images. My legs cramped, knots forming in the muscles as if they too rejected this torture. My fingers twitched, itching to lift the camera, to focus on something outside myself.

Then—nothing. A distant thunderclap rolled across the sky, and for one breath, the world contracted into silence. Leaves stilled, cicadas paused, the temple bells hung suspended in air. My mind stuttered and fell quiet, like a film abruptly cut. I tasted dust on my tongue, felt the pulse in my temples slow. For that single instant, the chatter stopped.

But the moment shattered as bells resumed their lament and pilgrims chanted sutras in unison. The noise felt both sacred and suffocating, drowning the fragile calm. I opened my eyes to see devotees circling the shrine, hands lifted, eyes closed. Ritual can be a crutch—or a cage.

I reached for my notebook, fingers shaking, and wrote:

"Stillness doesn't come by sitting—it comes by dropping the self you carry."

I pressed the pen harder, scoring the paper, the ink bleeding like truth through lies. My heart pounded; blood throbbed in my ears. I closed the book, sliding it under the stone. The Guide said tomorrow I would sit until the silence broke me—or I broke the silence.

My body screamed protest as I rose, legs unsteady, but my spirit felt a spark. I had tasted the void and lived to tell it. The path ahead was raw—no camera to shield me, no commentary to distract me. Only breath and bone, question and emptiness.

Night descended. Lanterns flickered; shadows danced on sacred walls. I stepped away from the tree, each footfall heavy with intention. Tomorrow, at first light, I would sit again. And perhaps, when the thunder spoke next, I would finally understand what he saw under this ancient canopy.

Chapter 4:

Beyond the Breaths

I don't know how long I sat there.

The monk's breaths had slowed, steady as the earth's pulse, while mine tangled in incense smoke and restless thoughts. His silence carried weight—not meditation anymore, but something deeper, somewhere I couldn't follow.

His chest rose and fell, like waves certain of their crash.

Then it stopped.

A slight slump, barely a shift. No gasp, no drama. Just stillness—clean, quiet, final. Like a curtain falling after a play no one noticed had ended.

It took me seconds to realize this wasn't meditation. It was death. The purest kind.

No one screamed. No one cried. They didn't see.

Pilgrims posed by statues, compared prayer beads, scrolled through apps promising "Inner Peace in 7 Steps." A man left the world, and they kept swiping.

I sat frozen, unsure if I should speak or stay, chasing the strange peace in that stillness. This wasn't the death I'd filmed—no blood, no claws, no cries. Just a body, empty of breath.

Maybe he chose this—to slip away without a stage.

A younger monk approached, whispered a prayer, checked his pulse, and draped the robe's edge over his face. No panic. No ritual. Just quiet acknowledgment.

One monk gone. Another would take his place. The world didn't flinch.

I stood, knees creaking. The sun had climbed, and the courtyard buzzed louder, as if drowning out the silence that had slipped through.

Death doesn't shock us when it's loud. It's the quiet ones—too clean, too real—that unsettle. No performance. Just the end.

That night, in a concrete room with a hard cot and no fan, I lay awake. A mosquito whined near my ear, competing with the temple's endless chants.

All I saw was that monk's last breath, soft as shedding a second skin. I saw a leopard cub in Ranthambore, throat torn by a rival, its cries fading in the dust. I saw a vulture pecking a still-breathing goat's eyes in the Himalayas. I saw a woman in a Himalayan village, TB-racked, smiling through her pain.

No death is beautiful. But some are honest.

That monk gave me my first.

The next morning, I woke before dawn. No shower—just cold water splashed on my face. I walked barefoot to the Bodhi Tree, not to ask, but to sit.

But the temple felt wrong.

They'd replaced him. The monk. His cushion still held his shape, but a younger one sat there, robes crisp, smile polished for Instagram pilgrims. The same chants droned. The same incense burned.

As if truth could be swapped for a fresher face.

A woman whispered to her child, "He's the real one, enlightened. See his glow?"

"Did he sit here yesterday?" the child asked.

"No," she said. "Yesterday's didn't smile."

So that's enlightenment now? A photo-op grin?

I nearly laughed, but it caught in my throat.

I turned away, needing distance from the temple's noise. In a dusty alley, I found a bookstore, its shelves sagging under forgotten tomes. The owner, eyes sharp despite his age, studied me.

"Got anything in Pali?" I asked.

He handed me a torn Dhammapada, wrapped in cloth. "His words," he said. "Not commentary. Not marketing. Just truth."

I sat on the floor, dust stinging my eyes, and read:

"All conditioned things are impermanent. When one sees this with wisdom, one turns away from suffering."

Simple. Brutal. Clean.

No promises of paradise. No salvation scams. Just truth: life decays, and wisdom is facing it.

I closed the book and wept—not from sadness, but from rage. Rage at how we'd turned his clarity into chants, his insight into currency, his stillness into selfies.

That night, I wrote in my journal:

"I didn't come to learn about the Buddha. I came to understand how we destroyed him."

Chapter 5:

The Last Possession

I returned to the Bodhi Tree before sunrise. The sky hung bruised purple, but the silence wasn't like yesterday's. That had breath, a living pulse. This was stiff—like a mouth sewn shut.

The monk's cushion was gone. An empty mat, swept too clean, lay in its place. Not a thread of him remained.

I sat anyway, pretending his space still held him. If I stayed still enough, maybe the air would whisper.

But silence doesn't lie. It held nothing.

Murmurs rose from the prayer halls, sharp words slicing through incense haze. I followed the noise.

Monks stood in a circle, robes loose in the heat, voices fraying. Not chanting—arguing.

"That almirah was his. He promised it to me."

"The begging bowl's mine. I carried it on his last yatra."

"He chose me for his cell."

"You're lying. I was closer."

A senior monk tried to hush them. They ignored him. One stormed off, shouting, "You want his legacy—his followers, his donations, his silence."

His silence. They wanted to own that too.

By mid-morning, word spread: Swami Dhanraj was coming.

His name drifted through ashrams like perfume masking rot. A man of

wealth, connections, cameras—blessing PR faster than sutras.
He arrived in a crisp white kurta, sunglasses defying the grey dawn. He bowed to the Bodhi Tree, then posed for a photographer, hands folded.
"A rare saint has left us," he declared. "We shall honor him."

Honor?
The outer yard transformed into a marketplace—plastic chairs, loudspeakers, banners with the monk's faded photo beside Dhanraj's high-resolution grin. A cardboard sign read:
Final Relics of the Silent Monk – Limited Blessings
Mala – ₹2,500
Used Cushion – ₹5,000
Private Meditation Slot – ₹10,000 (VIP Access Only)
A woman pressed her forehead to the monk's cushion, weeping into a scarf held by her driver. A man clutched the begging bowl, wrapped in gold cloth like a trophy. A teenager snapped a selfie with a "Blessed Robe."
The monk hadn't even been cremated.
They'd carved him up like sacred meat.

That night, I wrote in my journal: "This is the dharma now. Branding silence. Auctioning stillness. Holy men buried in hashtags."

Evening found me behind the main hall, far from the crowd. A young monk sat beside me, silent.
Then he spoke, voice trembling: "They're fighting over ashes, forgetting the fire."
He'd cared for the dead monk, maybe studied under him. He lit an incense stick, placing it on the cracked brick floor.
"I cleaned his body," he whispered. "He had nothing—no money, no will, no fear."
Tears glinted in his eyes. "They're building a museum. His death made him valuable."
I had no words, only anger and sorrow. My sister's book on Buddha, dog-eared and left behind, flashed in my mind—its truth now sold like that monk's robe.

Later, I opened the Dhammapada, desperate for calm. It mocked the world instead:
"Even a fine chariot decays. The body too. But the truth does not age."
I scribbled in the margins: They build a chariot from his corpse, riding it to the bank.
Then I wrote a poem, hand shaking:

The Last Possession
They strip your robe from your still chest,
Calling it a blessing.
Your bowl, where silence drank,
Now a miracle for sale.
Your cushion's gone. Your sandals sponsored.
Your name trademarked, your face on banners
You never wanted.
They chant your name louder now,
Not from love,
But to drown their guilt.
Truth has no place here.
Only relics. Only rituals.
Only the dead who can't speak back.

I closed the journal and decided.
I'd leave Bodh Gaya, carrying the monk's silence—not in robes or relics, but in the space he left behind.
He was the first true one I'd met. And the first they buried in noise.

Chapter 6:

The Leaving

I didn't speak for two days.

Not to the chai vendor, his cracked hands waving through steam. Not to the boy hawking prayer flags, their colors faded at the temple gates. My throat wasn't thirsty—it was sealed, refusing words.

The monk's death clung to me. Not just his stillness, but the auction that followed. They'd carved his silence into relics, branded it with prices, buried it under hashtags. And I—I stood there. Watched. Did nothing.

Guilt crept in like rot in a mango—sweet, then bitter, then choking. I tried the Bodhi Tree again, legs crossed on cracked stone. But the chants soured, the incense burned acrid. Tourists grinned for selfies by golden Buddhas, blind to the ghost of a monk who'd stopped breathing. His cushion was gone. So was the young monk who'd wept behind the hall. No one spoke of either.

They'd moved on.

I couldn't.

That night, nightmares peeled me open.

The monk's body, curled in a corner, flies on his lips. Swami Dhanraj looming, credit card reader glowing, a selfie-stick jutting from his ribs. My sister's book, dog-eared on her hospital bed, burned in a pile of relics.

I woke choking on spit, chest heaving. My camera lay by the bed, untouched. What would I shoot? Another fake smile? Another ritual for editors who'd never felt this weight?

The hotel manager knocked. Rent was due. I handed over my last rupees. He took them without a word—not cruel, just used to broken men leaving.

I wandered Bodh Gaya's alleys, shops screaming with trinkets, pilgrims heavier with offerings. A new monk sat on a fresh cushion, smiling for Instagram.

Then, in a back alley, I saw it—what I'd give anything to unsee.

Three monks, robes hiked to their knees, crouched over a heap: a cracked mala, a comb, the dead monk's robe. One flicked cigarette ash onto it, laughing. "He don't need it now."

The robe—the one he wore when he exhaled truth.

Now it soaked up spit.

I vomited behind a rusted scooter, bile burning my throat, clinging to my teeth.

Evening found me on the guesthouse roof, sky black and unyielding. No chants. No lights. Just stars, sharp as accusations.

I opened the torn Dhammapada, its pages brittle. A line stabbed me:

"This world is blind. Few are those who see."

I laughed—or sobbed. They bled together.

In my journal, I scratched: "The world isn't blind. It's drunk on its own eyes."

Then, harder, ink tearing the page: "He died for silence. They sold it. I let it happen."

Thunder cracked past midnight, a scream that matched mine. For once, the world wasn't smiling.

I didn't pack right. Just shoved clothes into my bag, like burying a body. Left the tripod, the filters, the wide lens I once loved. Too heavy for a world this small.

One last walk through the temple gate.

A woman in a tattered sari lit a butter lamp, its flame trembling against the wind. No selfies, no blessings—just grief, quiet and unbranded. A name on her lips, maybe a son, maybe a husband. She cupped the flame with both hands, shielding it like a heart.

I watched longer than I'd watched anything since the monk.

My sister's book flashed in my mind—her voice reading Buddha's words, now drowned by this temple's noise. I'd failed her truth, just like I'd failed his silence.

I turned away. No goodbye.

A one-way bus ticket to Sarnath, where Buddha first spoke truth, weighed in my pocket. Notebook in hand, haunted by silence, I left.

Not for peace.

If I stayed, I'd become the noise.

Chapter 7:

First Sermons, Last Illusions

The road to Sarnath wasn't long, but inside me, something tore—cracked like wet bark under a merciless sun. I didn't look out the bus window. Didn't need to. The world outside was already in my skull: temples pimped like theme parks, monks with corporate grins, dust choking statues of truth.

I arrived empty. Not the monk's stillness from Bodh Gaya. Just… gutted. Like someone scooped out my voice, my faith, my sister's book—left on her hospital bed—and abandoned the skin to stumble on.

Sarnath. Where Buddha spoke his first truth. Where deer once heard silence as language.

Now—LED signboards blaring mantra apps. Rickshaws wrapped in Om decals. A replica stupa polished like a showroom car. A gift shop, "Dhammachakra Delights," peddling "I Found My Path" t-shirts.

No, you didn't. You bought a lie.

A tour guide, lanyard gleaming, fake British accent dripping, waved me to a group. I shook him off, found a cracked wall, and sat, legs crossed against stone. A stray dog slept nearby, twitching in dreams. I envied its peace.

My journal crinkled—sweat, rain, guilt. I scratched without thinking:

"They sell his words in packets. Chant truth to drown it. Teach freedom like a syllabus. Every disciple with a business card."

I slammed it shut, ink bleeding like my sister's book, now dust in a world of hashtags.

A man in saffron robes glided past, cloth too clean, too bright. He walked like he knew cameras followed, even if none did. Foreigners trailed him, whispering "Swami Vimalakirti"—a name stolen from Mahāyāna texts, nothing true about it.

I shadowed them to a marble building, "The House of First Truth." Golden walls, digital donation machines, AC vents humming like locusts. A plaque lied: Dedicated to the Living Lineage of Enlightened Ones.

Vimalakirti sat on a dais, microphone clipped, camera crew fussing with lights. His smile was all marketing, no soul.

"My children," he purred, "we don't worship Buddha—we become Buddha."

Applause. Plastic chairs groaned. A woman wept.

He raised a hand. "The body is a distraction. Truth lies in giving. Donate with love."

QR codes flashed on a projector, glinting like vulture eyes.

I couldn't breathe. This wasn't teaching—it was trafficking. Mugging Buddha's corpse for profit.

A foreigner in the crowd stared at me, my clenched fists, my scowl. "You see it too?" she whispered. I didn't answer, fleeing the marble cage for air.

Outside, real ruins—stone worn by time, not hashtags' acid rain. A cracked pillar bore a Pali inscription, raw and human, no polish. I couldn't read it, but it felt true.

Sunset bled behind the stupas. I wandered to a rusted fence, where monument met dirt. A boy drew in the dust with a stick—Dharmachakra, uneven, alive.

"Why the wheel?" I asked.

He shrugged. "Teacher says truth keeps moving."

The words hit harder than Vimalakirti's sermon. Truth moves. They'd pinned it, embalmed it in gold, charged for a peek.

"Where's your teacher?"

He pointed to a shack beyond the fence. "She teaches under a neem tree. Says Buddha hated temples. Wanted thinking."

I smiled, first time since Bodh Gaya's butter lamp. A flicker of fire they hadn't smothered.

That night, I sat under her neem tree, alone. Moonlight cracked through clouds. My journal opened, and I wrote:

"Buddha never asked to be followed. He begged us to see. The blind wrote scriptures. The mute became preachers. Truth didn't die in Bodh Gaya—it bleeds here too."

I didn't meditate. Just sat, still, burning. Someone watched from the shadows—a pilgrim, maybe, drawn to my silence. I ignored them.

Truth keeps moving. I'd follow it to Kushinagar, where Buddha left his body. Maybe there, I'd find what Sarnath buried.

Chapter 8:

Where Truth Dies

Kushinagar reeked of wet leaves, diesel, and rot—like time itself had soured, left to fester.

I arrived half-starved, half-mad, silence strangling my throat like a noose. The bus coughed black into the sky and wheezed away. Ahead—fog, flickering temple lights, tourists buzzing like flies.

This was where Buddha died.

A guide chirped, "Here, the great one attained Mahāparinirvāṇa," pointing at a reclining Buddha statue—too golden, too polished, too at peace.

No peace in me. Just rot.

Rituals choked the air. A man sold garlands outside the Parinirvana Temple, hands stained yellow from stale marigold. "For liberation, sir," he said.

Liberation? I was still choking on Bodh Gaya's ash, Sarnath's applause.

My boots squelched mud and bone dust. A procession passed—monks with selfie sticks, tourists in yoga pants humming half-learned mantras. I slipped down a side path, away from their noise.

Behind the temple, a cremation site. Not for Buddha—his flames were centuries gone—but for the forgotten. Smoke curled from a crumbling pyre. Two men squatted, poking a burning corpse's ribs like they were turning meat.

No chants. No doctrine. Just death, naked and raw.

I sat, nose burning, smoke stinging my eyes. This was the sermon—fire, flesh, inevitability. Not starlight, not awakening. Bones hiss. Truth blackens.

The man burning—no name, maybe a beggar, maybe a father. Tossed like garbage onto the fire. No relics, no sellers. Just the end.

My journal shook in my hands:

"Buddha died here. So did this man. One gets garlands, the other flies."

"They say he broke the cycle. I say he just left. And they couldn't stand it."

A boy, ash-smeared, eyes like storm clouds, stood beside me. "You writing about him?"

I nodded.

"Was he someone?"

I shook my head.

"Don't waste your ink," he said, barefoot, vanishing into smoke.

That night, I lay on a guesthouse mattress, thin as grief, walls stained with piss, fan clicking like a countdown. The burning clung to me—the boy's voice, cold and final: He's already gone.

But what if no one truly goes? What if we're just stories for the next lie?

My sister's book, dog-eared on her hospital bed, flashed in my mind. Buddha said no idols, no worship. They built a hundred thousand. He said look inward; they built temples outward. Now Kushinagar sold tickets to death.

I whispered, "What if they do this to me? Sell my camera, my journal, my silence?"

I wept—not for myself, not for Buddha, but for truth, beaten until it smiled.

Morning broke like a scar.

I wandered the ruins—bricks melted by monsoon, staircases to nowhere. No brochures, no performances.

An old woman swept the path, back bent like a question mark. "Looking for Buddha?"

"Maybe."

"He's not here," she smirked. "He left. They forgot to leave with him."

A conch sounded from a hut, pulling me like prey. Inside, a blind man sat, no statues, no altar—just smoke and silence.

"You carry something heavy," he said, eyes unopened.

"Truth."

He smiled. "Then it's not yours. Let it go."

I wanted to scream, but I sat, breathing his tea's warmth. No wisdom, no sermon—just honesty.

That night, I wrote:

"They burned him here. He let them. They built temples he'd never enter. Legends he'd refuse."

"Truth isn't light or awakening—it's the courage to vanish without legacy."

I whispered my sister's name, nearly forgotten. I'd failed her again, chasing truth in a world that sold it. But Kushinagar's silence didn't care. It was honest, not holy.

Someone watched from the shadows—a pilgrim, maybe, drawn to my journal's scratch. I turned away.

Kushinagar wasn't the end. I'd carry its smoke to the next place—maybe a gurdwara, where Nanak's truth might still breathe.

Chapter 9:

Langar and the Silence Between

The road to the gurdwara sliced through mustard fields, alive with silence—not Bodh Gaya's branded hush, not Kushinagar's death-hiss, but a wound scabbed over, still raw.

The bus dumped me on a cracked highway outside Amritsar, a peeling sign whispering: "ੴ – There is One God." My boots blistered, bag light, journal more scar than paper.

The gurdwara stood plain—white walls, no LED lies, no monks grinning for cameras. Kirtan hummed low, not selling, just breathing.

I shed my shoes, draped a borrowed scarf over my head. No one stared. No selfie-sticks. No price tags. A man swept marble with a jhadu, pausing to smile at a fly buzzing his ear—his seva, his prayer.

I sat, cross-legged, at the back. No statues, just the Guru Granth Sahib under a canopy, words sung, not owned. Truth as sound, not property.

A boy, maybe twelve, hummed off-key, breaking karah prasad in half. "Sweet?" he asked, handing me a piece.

I nodded, tasting more than sugar—something untainted, unlike Bodh Gaya's ash or Sarnath's applause. My sister's voice whispered: "If there's truth, it must feed the hungry."

In the langar hall, I sat on the floor with laborers, women, a man with no legs. Steel plates clinked. Daal spilled from a ladle, no questions asked. A woman in a faded salwar grinned wide as history. “No one goes hungry here.”

No caste, no creed, no cameras. Just food, dignity, equality.

I wept into my chapati, quietly. No one asked why. They let me.

Guru Nanak’s truth burned—not through scripture, but action: Naam Japna, remember the Name; Kirat Karni, earn honestly; Vand Chakna, share with all.

He walked with farmers, spoke to Sufis, dined with outcasts. Never called himself holy. Just listened. When priests sold heaven, he gave truth for free.

“There is no Hindu. No Muslim. Only the human.”

They tried to silence him. Fought over his body—burn or bury? Morning came, only flowers remained.

Night fell, stars sharp as accusations. I sat outside, crickets mingling with clanging langar pots.

A sevadar paused, turban loose, palms dusted with flour. “Staying tonight?”

I nodded.

“You seem heavy,” he said, sitting beside me.

I clutched my journal, fearing it’d be sold one day, like my sister’s book, like Nanak’s words on “Chardi Kala” t-shirts.

“You don’t have to believe anything,” he said. “Just eat. Sleep. Help. Heal.”

“Even without God?”

He brushed a mosquito off his arm, smiling. “Service is God enough.”

My sister's voice echoed: Feed the hungry. This fed me.

But I didn't trust it.

I'd seen truth rot—Bodh Gaya's relics, Sarnath's QR codes, Kushinagar's garlands. Even this purity could turn to gold-plated kirpans, guru keychains.

Not here, not yet. This gurdwara held Nanak's silence.

I wrote:

"Some silence feeds you. Some devours. Nanak spoke through hunger, not dogma. He didn't say 'Follow me.' He said, Feed them."

A shadow moved—someone watching my pen's scratch, drawn to my quiet. I ignored them.

I slept on a jute mat, fan clicking like truth unraveling. Tomorrow, north—Dharamsala, maybe, where mountains might hold something unbranded.

Tonight, I was almost human. Nanak's gift: not salvation, but the unbearable dignity of being.

Chapter 10:

Smoke Over Cedars

Dharamsala rose like a ghost through mist—bone-cold, indifferent, cedars whispering warnings, not prayers.

I arrived starved, not of food, but belief. The gurdwara's warmth (Chapter 9) faded like my sister's book, dog-eared on her hospital bed. Hope was a lie the body tells to survive another dawn.

The bus clawed up the mountain, pines looming. Valleys gaped below like fresh wounds. Snow waited above, ready to bury.

I stepped into silence—not staged, not sacred, just wind cutting through bruised cedars. Nature endures, doesn't chant.

Lower streets choked with tourists—white dreadlocks, gemstone stalls, neon signs peddling "Tibetan Peace Massages" and "Karma Cafes." Enlightenment in soy candles. A sign read: Breathe in the Mountain. Exhale the Ego.

They exhaled nothing. Just swallowed more.

I climbed slick stone steps, moss underfoot, air thinning, cleaner, fiercer. A monk passed, robes dusty, eyes hollow. I didn't nod back—tired of masks after Bodh Gaya's relics, Sarnath's QR codes, Kushinagar's garlands.

At the peak, clouds bled into trees. No hashtags, no selfies—just breath, rain's threat, cedar's ache.

On a crumbling ledge, I overlooked the valley: hotels sprouting like tumors, roads gouging silence's roots. Plastic garlands snagged in pines. A rock screamed FREE TIBET in spray paint, a Coke can abandoned beside it.

They didn't want freedom. They wanted souvenirs.

My journal, curled from rain and grief, shook as I wrote:

"Mountains can't breathe. Trees hang like prisoners, roots gagged by concrete. We climb to conquer, to post, to brand. Nature's the last unpriced thing. But we'll price it. We always do."

Rain slapped down, cold, alive. I didn't move, soaked to the bone, my sister's words drowning in this world's noise.

A man on the trail shouted into a Bluetooth noose: "Bro, I'm on a spiritual detox, ya know?"—then bit a protein bar.

A Tibetan tea shack offered warmth. The owner, eyes like glaciers, poured without words. Steam curled, real as incense but unbranded.

"Pilgrim?" he asked, eyeing my journal.

"Something like that."

He stared past me, into rain-thick trees. "The gods left. Only echoes now."

"We burned them with the forests," I said.

He poured more tea.

Night fell in a crooked guesthouse, wind clawing windows, a rat scratching walls. It wasn't pretending—I liked that.

At dawn, the Dalai Lama's temple stood empty. No chants, just mops dragging across marble. A monk lit butter lamps, one by one, small flames against a darkening world.

Under a scarred pine—initials carved deep, P + R = Forever—I wrote:

"They call these mountains holy, but we poison every peak. Temples rise for signal, not God. Pilgrims pose, not pray. They don't know faith. They know algorithms."

A child skipped past, spinning a wooden wheel. "What are you writing?"

"What people forget."

She nodded, too young to understand, but her eyes held a spark.

A shadow lingered—a pilgrim, maybe, watching my journal's scratch, drawn to my silence. I turned away, fearing they'd sell its pages one day, like my camera, like my sister's book.

Dharamsala wasn't the end. Another ruin waited—incense, receipts, lies. But tonight, I stayed with the cedars, not for healing, but to witness.

Truth isn't a path. Sometimes, it's just a place to burn quietly—before they pave it too.

Chapter 11:

Truth Without a Tongue

I didn't speak for three days. Grief sewed my mouth shut—not holy, not meditation, just silence bleeding out.

Dharamsala's cedar and diesel clung to my jacket. I hitched south through dust-stained towns peddling truth in jars—crystals, "soul-aligned" ayurveda, Instagrammable asceticism. No one walked. They posed.

Mountains faded, but their ache stayed, sharp as my sister's book, lost to a world of banners and broken gods.

A rickshaw driver pointed to an ashram in a nameless town. "Foreigners love it. Guru's got a podcast." Of course he did.

Barefoot, I entered—marble gleaming, sage smoke curling, OM cushions made in China. A guru, face frozen like a Botox Buddha, preached love, surrender, divine integration. Then the pitch: QR codes, courses, "awakening" for $108/month.

"Spirituality is your birthright," he purred, "but community costs."

Bile rose like prayer turned sour. I fled before the donation bowls, stomach churning as in Bodh Gaya's alleys.

Outside, dusk's ash settled. A woman swept the gate, cracked nails coughing dust. No smile, no show—just knowing eyes.

I sat beside her, silent.

"Do you listen to the guru?" I asked.

She swept on, dust coiling like incense no one would buy. "I hear the broom more."

That night, in a guesthouse with mildew creeping like grief, I scribbled:

"They brand the silence. Sell it. But the broom speaks louder."

I dreamt of my sister, walking away through mud and shattered statues. I ran, called her name—no mouth, just wind where a voice should be.

Morning broke in the city square. Influencers set up ring lights, one in saffron robes like a costume, another sipping green juice between takes, rehearsing "authenticity."

One noticed me, maybe from some viral corner of Sarnath or Kushinagar. "You a seeker?" he asked, phone angled at his jawline.

"No."

"Share your journey on camera?"

"My journey's a funeral," I said. "You're dancing on the corpse."

He grinned. "Perfect line. Can I use it?"

A crowd glanced over, drawn to my voice, my journal's weight. I walked away, heart pounding.

At the town's edge, a ruined structure—columns broken, paint peeled, no sermons. A wall bore a red smear—blood, maybe a dog's, maybe a man's.

I sat, journal trembling:

"Truth has no address. It sits in filth, in failed words, in broken gods. The mouthless scream outlasts mantras."

Wind swept in, cold, real, unsellable.

A man stood in the archway, camera raised. Not a pilgrim—a vulture. I raised my hand—gently, firmly—no.

He lowered it, but I knew: one day, they'd raise it again. After I'm gone, after I fall, they'd sell my journal's pages, my camera's lens, my silence as scripture.

Even if I beg:

"I am not a teacher. I am not a path. I am not a name."

They'll name me anyway.

That night, no lamp, just darkness staring back.

Tomorrow, east—to a Sufi shrine, where an imam's silence might still breathe under a broken dome.

Not to pray. Not to teach. To listen—one last time, before they burn that too.

Chapter 12:

Whispers Under the Shrine

Dusk bled into evening as I reached the Sufi shrine—a dome of peeling gold, shadows pooling like spilled ink. No QR codes, no guidebooks, no influencers in borrowed robes. Just a ragged door and silence thick enough to choke.

Inside, sandalwood clung to cracked walls. A trembling lamp lit a faded portrait: Sarmad Kashani, eyes wild, beard braided in defiance. Tiles bore names—Bulleh Shah, Sheikh Farid, Mian Mir, Peer Buddhu Shah—souls who spoke to khuda without screens or sermons.

I knelt on cold stone, heart hollow, my sister's book a ghost in my bag, its pages as lost as her voice. I'd come for truth beyond temple lies—untamed, unpriced.

A caretaker, robed in dust, settled beside me, silent as a shadow. He lit incense, smoke curling for God, not show.

"They killed Sarmad for truth," I whispered. "Naked, no sect, no temple."

He nodded. "He stood bare for God. Better than clothed for profit."

His voice cracked: "They feared he'd snap their chains."

I saw the ashram's guru—Bodh Gaya's relics, Sarnath's QR codes, Kushinagar's garlands, Amritsar's t-shirts, Dharamsala's cafes. New thieves, same theft.

He pointed to a dusty alcove: men chanted, cross-legged, no mics, no applause. Just words passing like breath between hearts.

Words glowed on broken stone:

"Bulleh Shah: I am not in the mosque, nor in the temple."

"Sheikh Farid: Let the heart be a temple."

"Mian Mir: I laid the Golden Temple's stone—no boundary between faiths."

"Peer Buddhu Shah: He stood with Guru Gobind Singh Ji, died for him, gave his sons to fight at Bhangani."

Truth lived, not sold.

"Why stay?" I asked a chanter, voice soft.

Eyes closed, he said, "We don't sell. We remember."

His words cracked through smoke like a prayer's end. A quiet rebellion.

Night deepened, stars piercing the cracked dome. I scribbled:

"Truth lives in shadows. It doesn't ask for likes, doesn't beg for follows. It bleeds, sings, dies naked."

The caretaker handed me a tarnished coin—Sarmad's, unbranded. "Keep it," he whispered. "Don't speak its worth."

I pressed it to my chest, warm as my sister's fading voice.

A shadow moved—a crowd, eyes on my journal, my silence. They'd sell it one day—my pages, my camera, my grief as scripture.

Even if I beg: "I am not a teacher. I am not a path."

They'll name me anyway.

Tomorrow, the city—Delhi, maybe, or Bodh Gaya's ashes. The last stage, where they'll raise stones, tear me apart in temples and tweets, sell my silence as a sermon.

But maybe someone will hold this coin, not for its price, but its pulse.

I'd go east, to where truth might still breathe under a broken dome. Not to pray, but to listen—before they burn that too.

Chapter 13:

The City's Teeth

Delhi chewed me up before I stepped off the bus—smog like ash in my lungs, billboards screaming lies into the dawn. Awaken Your Destiny: Join Now. Acharya Rudra's face, airbrushed to godhood, grinned from every corner, his eyes glinting like coins.

I was starved—not of bread, but belief. The scars of Bodh Gaya's relics, Sarnath's QR codes, Kushinagar's burning corpse, Amritsar's langar, Dharamsala's poisoned peaks, the Sufi shrine's cracked dome—they'd carved me hollow. My sister's book, dog-eared on her hospital bed, weighed heavier than my journal, its pages curling like a wound that wouldn't close.

The bus spat me into a street pulsing with hawkers—sacred threads, plastic Buddhas, "blessed" roses for a price. A neon sign blinked: Rudra's Nirvana App – Download Your Peace. This wasn't a city. It was a mouth, teeth sharpened on truth's bones.

At a chai stall, men whispered of Rudra's empire—ashrams, apps, relic markets trafficking stolen stones and fake scrolls. My fist clenched around Sarmad's tarnished coin, its pulse the last real thing I held. Rage, raw as bile, rose from Bodh Gaya's ashes. Rudra wasn't just a fraud—he was the king of thieves, weaving Buddha's truths, Nanak's service, and Sufi songs into a net of profit.

I wandered to Hazrat Nizamuddin's dargah, its courtyard a fleeting refuge from Delhi's growl. A qawwali singer, blind and weathered, sang without a mic—voice cracking like stone under time, not chasing likes. He sang of Nizamuddin Auliya, who fed the poor while emperors hoarded gold. "Rudra's men come now," he muttered, "selling roses for salvation."

I clutched the coin, its warmth my sister's ghost. "They sell everything," I said.

He nodded. "Even God."

A marigold vendor, barely twenty, eyes heavy with hunger, stared at me. "Baba," she whispered, "bless me." My face—maybe from Sarnath's outburst or Kushinagar's scribbled grief—had spread, a viral shadow.

"I'm no saint," I snapped, voice breaking. "No teacher, no path."

She knelt anyway, touching my boots. A crowd gathered, murmuring "prophet," eyes on my journal, my camera. I fled, heart pounding—they were already carving me into their messiah.

Purana Qila's ruins loomed—Mughal stones crumbling under smog and neglect. There, Acharya Rudra held court, a pop-up satsang streamed to millions. His voice, slick as oil, wove Buddha's Four Noble Truths, Nanak's Vand Chakna, Sarmad's naked defiance into a pitch: "Join my tribe, awaken your soul—first month free."

Cameras glinted like vulture eyes. My hands shook, journal heavy as a stone. I shouted, "Truth isn't an app! You can't sell what bleeds!"

The crowd froze. Rudra smiled, predatory, and beckoned me to the stage. "A seeker of fire," he purred, "join us, share your light."

I spat, "You're a thief, stealing gods for clicks."

Gasps. Phones rose, flashing, framing me as their savior, their rebel. Rudra's eyes narrowed—he saw profit in my rage, a new face for his brand.

I ran, boots pounding cracked earth, into the shadow of a banyan tree, its roots strangling stone like Delhi's greed. Alone, I wrote:

"They'll sell my scream, my silence, my sister's ghost. Truth isn't a coin—it's a wound that bleeds forever."

I dreamt of her, face blurred, holding my camera, its lens burning her hands. A mob chanted my name, raising my journal like scripture. I woke, gasping, Sarmad's coin cutting my palm.

Rudra's empire would hunt me—exploit or erase. Tomorrow, I'd face his heart: his mega-ashram, his relic market, his lies. Not to save anyone. To scream one last time—before the city's teeth closed.

I whispered my sister's name, the coin's pulse against my heart. Truth wasn't here. But I'd chase its echo, even if it killed me.

Chapter 14:

The Ashram's Hunger

Delhi's smog devoured the stars, leaving only Rudra's billboards to blaze—neon vultures promising eternity for a swipe. His mega-ashram squatted at the city's edge, a glass shrine to greed, its gates sharp as jaws.

I stood outside, Sarmad's coin slicing my palm, my sister's ghost heavier than my journal. The scars of Bodh Gaya's stolen relics, Sarnath's digital prayers, Kushinagar's burning corpse, Amritsar's langar, Dharamsala's poisoned peaks, the Sufi shrine's cracked dome—they'd carved me raw. Acharya Rudra, the serpent of profit, had spun Buddha's truths, Nanak's service, Nizamuddin's qawwali into a web of lies, selling salvation like street meat.

My camera hung like a chain around my neck. My scream at Purana Qila—calling him a thief—had gone viral, my face now a pixelated ghost: The Rebel Seeker. Crowds trailed me, whispering "baba," their eyes ravenous for a savior I'd never be.

I slipped past guards in starched kurtas, their smiles cutting like glass. Inside, the ashram throbbed—followers in saffron robes, smartwatches blinking, minds dulled by Rudra's app. A screen looped his sermon: "Surrender your soul, join my tribe—premium unlocks divinity."

Bile burned my throat, sour as prayers sold cheap. A man in a tailored dhoti, clutching a "sacred" QR-coded wristband, grabbed me. "You're the one," he hissed, "the rebel who spoke truth." His phone flashed, stealing my shadow. Others turned, cameras glinting like vulture eyes, chanting my name as if it were a mantra.

I tore free, boots pounding marble, into a corridor of relics—fake bones labeled Buddha's, forged verses branded Nanak's, Sufi coins polished to lies. A glass case held a t-shirt, too close to mine, tagged Relic of the Fire-Bearer. My journal shook in my bag, my sister's book a ghost beside it. They'd sell my breath before it stopped.

A door opened to a courtyard, where Rudra lounged on a velvet throne, livestreaming to millions. His voice slithered, honey and venom: "Truth is a transaction—subscribe, ascend, belong."

He was no guru—just a mirror of the world's greed, turning faith into a slot machine. I stepped forward, gravel crunching. "You're a parasite," I roared, "chewing gods to spit coins!"

The crowd froze, phones rising like a swarm. Rudra's eyes gleamed—not with anger, but hunger. "A voice of fire," he purred, "join us, light our path."

"Truth doesn't stream," I spat. "It bleeds!"

His guards lunged, but the crowd surged, clawing for my journal, my camera, my t-shirt. "Baba! Save us!" A woman tore my sleeve, another kissed my boots, their worship a blade at my throat. I saw it—my death, not in peace, but in pieces, my words twisted into apps, my face on billboards.

I ran, through halls plastered with Rudra's grin, into an alley where Delhi's pulse thrashed—diesel, sweat, rot. Under a dying streetlamp, I wrote:

"They'll carve my bones into apps, my screams into subscriptions. Truth isn't a signal—it's a wound the world won't let heal."

I dreamt of my sister, her face fading, stitching my t-shirt into a shroud. A mob raised my camera, its lens dripping blood, chanting my name like a curse. I woke, gasping, Sarmad's coin slick with sweat, my sister's whisper—Truth feeds the hungry—a knife in my chest.

Rudra's empire saw me now—his enforcers would hunt, his followers would deify. Tomorrow, I'd storm his relic market, the belly of his lies, to tear it down or burn with it. Not for redemption. For the echo of her voice, fading in this city's teeth.

The coin pulsed against my heart. I was no saint, but I'd scream until my blood ran dry—before they sold my silence too.

Chapter 15:

The Market of Bones

Delhi's heart pulsed with rot—alleys choked with diesel fumes, streetlights flickering like dying prayers. Rudra's relic market sprawled in the city's gut, a bazaar of stolen gods. Stalls glittered with fake relics—Buddha's teeth, Nanak's beads, Sufi coins polished to lies. My face, now a viral curse from the ashram's chaos, stared from posters: The Fire-Bearer, Live Stream Tonight.

I was no saint, but they'd carved me into one. Sarmad's coin burned in my pocket, my sister's ghost heavier than my journal, its pages curling like her hospital bed's sheets. Bodh Gaya's relic auctions, Sarnath's QR codes, Kushinagar's burning corpse, Amritsar's langar, Dharamsala's poisoned peaks, the Sufi shrine's cracked dome, Rudra's velvet throne—they'd led me here, to the belly of the beast.

My camera dangled, a noose around my neck. The crowd's chants from the ashram—"Baba! Save us!"—echoed, their worship a blade at my throat. Rudra's enforcers would hunt me now, their eyes glinting like the vulture cameras of his followers.

I slipped into the market, past hawkers peddling "sacred" threads and plastic malas. A stall sold t-shirts printed with my face, captioned Voice of Truth. My stomach twisted—my sister's book, my journal, my t-shirt, all fodder for their greed. A vendor offered me tea, its steam curling like incense, but I tasted venom in its heat, a bitter tang of poison. I spat it out, heart pounding. Rudra's reach was deeper than I'd feared.

In the market's core, a stage rose, draped in saffron and LED lights. Rudra stood, a predator in silk, auctioning a "relic" of me—a torn scrap of my t-shirt, stained with alley dirt. "The Fire-Bearer's essence," he crowed, "bid now, claim divinity!" The crowd roared, hands waving phones, their bids a fevered prayer.

Chapter 16:

The Scream That Breaks

Delhi's veins pulsed with decay—warehouses sagging under smog, their shadows swallowing the last of the light. Rudra's syndicate core hid here, a labyrinth of servers and stolen gods, spinning lies into code. My face, now a cursed icon from the relic market's chaos, flickered on cracked screens: The Fire-Bearer, Live to Liberate.

I was no saint, just a wound bleeding truth. Sarmad's coin burned in my pocket, my sister's ghost heavier than my journal, its pages fraying like her hospital bed's sheets. Bodh Gaya's relic auctions, Sarnath's QR codes, Kushinagar's burning corpse, Amritsar's langar, Dharamsala's poisoned peaks, the Sufi shrine's cracked dome, Rudra's ashram and market—they'd carved me raw. My camera, a noose around my neck, caught the mob's chants: "Baba! Save us!" Their worship was a blade, and Rudra's enforcers were sharpening it.

I'd tasted poison in the market's tea, seen the vial in an enforcer's hand. Rudra knew I'd screamed his truth—called him a leech, a thief of gods. Tonight, I'd expose him, rip his empire's mask, even if it tore me apart.

I slipped into the warehouse, past guards with eyes like knives, their kurtas stained with diesel and greed. Inside, servers hummed, screens glowing with Rudra's lies—fake relics, forged scriptures, my own t-shirt sold as a Relic of the Fire-Bearer. A ledger lay open: profits from Bodh Gaya's stones, Sarnath's scrolls, Nizamuddin's roses. My hands shook, rage raw as blood.

A back room held Rudra's archive—photos of his empire, deals with relic smugglers, bank accounts bloated with stolen faith. I found a video file: Rudra laughing, admitting his fraud. "Truth is a product," he sneered, "and I'm its king." My camera burned against my chest—I recorded the screen, his confession a scream to shatter his throne.

Voices echoed. I uploaded the video to a public server, my fingers trembling, the coin's pulse my only anchor. It spread—phones buzzing, screens lighting up across Delhi: Rudra Exposed.

I ran, boots pounding concrete, into a yard where Rudra stood, his silk robes gleaming under floodlights. A crowd gathered, phones raised, my video playing on their screens. "He's a fraud!" I roared, voice cracking like stone. "He sells your gods, your souls!"

Rudra's smile faltered, eyes venomous. "A lost soul," he called, "spreading lies to divide us." But the crowd wavered, murmurs rising—some threw their malas, others clutched my name like a prayer.

An enforcer lunged, his vial glinting—poison, meant to silence me. I dodged, but the mob surged, splitting into chaos: some chanting "Baba! Truth!" others screaming "Traitor!" A fist grazed my jaw, a hand tore my t-shirt. My journal fell, pages scattering like ash. I grabbed it, camera swinging, and fled into the city's maw.

Under a rusted water tower, I crouched, journal bleeding ink:

"I broke his mask, but they'll break me. Truth isn't a video—it's a wound no signal can hold."

I dreamt of my sister, her face fading, stitching my t-shirt into a crown. A mob raised my camera, its lens weeping blood, chanting my name like a noose. I woke, choking, Sarmad's coin cutting my palm, her whisper—Truth feeds the hungry—a shard in my lungs.

Rudra's empire was cracking, but his enforcers were closer, their poison vials gleaming. The mob, split between worship and rage, would tear me apart. Tomorrow, I'd face his final stronghold—his server hub, his lies' heart—to burn it or die. Not for glory. For her echo, fading in this city of knives.

The coin pulsed, warm as my blood. I wasn't a prophet, but I'd scream until my bones broke—before they sold my death as scripture.

I climbed the stage, boots grinding filth. "You're selling lies!" I screamed, voice raw as blood. "Truth isn't a relic—it's a wound!"

The crowd stilled, then erupted, clawing for me. "Baba! Bless us!" A woman seized my journal, another tore my camera strap. I fought free, but a man in Rudra's kurta slipped close, his breath sour with intent. "Join or die," he hissed, a vial glinting in his hand—poison, meant for me.

I ran, alleys swallowing me, their walls scrawled with my name in paint and prayer. Under a broken bridge, I crouched, journal trembling:

"They'll grind my bones to apps, my blood to streams. Truth isn't a bid—it's a scream no one hears."

I dreamt of my sister, her face fading, weaving my t-shirt into a noose. A mob raised my journal, its pages bleeding ink, chanting my name like a chain. I woke, choking, Sarmad's coin slick with sweat, my sister's whisper—Truth feeds the hungry—a blade in my ribs.

Rudra's market wasn't the end. His syndicate sprawled deeper—warehouses, servers, lies spun into code. Tomorrow, I'd find his core, burn his empire or choke on its ashes. Not for salvation. For her echo, fading in this market of bones.

The coin pulsed, warm as blood. I wasn't a prophet, but I'd scream until my veins ran dry—before they sold my death too.

Chapter 17:

The Hunt's Shadow

Delhi's underbelly bled—gutters thick with oil, air heavy with ash. Rudra's empire, cracked by my video exposing his fraud, hunted me now, its servers humming lies in hidden warehouses. My face, a viral wound, glared from posters: The Fire-Bearer, Savior or Traitor?

I was no saint, just a scream choking on truth. Sarmad's coin burned in my pocket, hot as my fading blood, my sister's ghost heavier than my journal, its pages fraying like her hospital bed's sheets. Bodh Gaya's relic auctions, Sarnath's QR codes, Kushinagar's burning corpse, Amritsar's langar, Dharamsala's poisoned peaks, the Sufi shrine's cracked dome, Rudra's ashram and market—they'd torn me raw. My camera, a noose around my neck, caught the mob's chants: "Baba! Truth!" and "Traitor! Liar!"

The exposure had split them—half worshipped me, half wanted my blood. Rudra's enforcers, vials glinting with poison, wanted my silence. I tasted their venom in the market's tea, saw it in their eyes at the ashram. My scream had broken Rudra's mask, but it painted a target on my chest.

I hid in an alley, its walls scrawled with my name in paint and curses. A street vendor, eyes hollow, offered me bread. I refused—poison lingered in every cup, every crumb. "Baba," he whispered, "save us." I shook my head, voice cracking. "I'm no savior. Just a wound."

He knelt anyway, touching my boots. A crowd gathered, some praying, others spitting, their phones flashing like vulture eyes. A woman tore at my t-shirt, another grabbed for my journal. I shoved through, heart pounding, their worship and rage a blade at my throat.

I fled to a derelict temple, its spire crumbling like my hope. Inside, no idols—just dust and echoes. I leaned against a cracked pillar, journal trembling:

"They'll tear me like hyenas, vultures ripping flesh. No grave, just scraps sold as scripture. Truth isn't a stream—it's a wound bleeding dry."

I dreamt of my sister, her face fading, stitching my t-shirt into a shroud. Hyenas and vultures tore at my body, my camera's lens weeping blood, my journal's pages scattered like ash. A mob chanted my name, half in worship, half in wrath. I woke, choking, Sarmad's coin cutting my palm, her whisper—Truth feeds the hungry—a knife in my chest.

Footsteps echoed. An enforcer stood in the temple's archway, vial glinting, his kurta stained with Delhi's rot. "Rudra wants you," he hissed. "Join or die."

I ran, through alleys thick with smog, toward Rudra's server hub—the heart of his lies. Tomorrow, I'd burn it or bleed trying. Not for salvation. For her echo, fading in this city of claws.

The coin burned, hot as my fading blood. I'm no savior, but I'll scream until my bones shatter—before they tear me apart like vultures.

Chapter 18:

The Noose of Eyes

Delhi's smog clawed the sky, a shroud over a city that devoured its own. Rudra's server hub loomed in the distance, a steel heart pumping lies, its wires strangling truth. My exposure—his confession, my scream—had cracked his empire, but the wound was mine. Posters of my face, The Fire-Bearer, Savior or Traitor?, bled across walls, my name a curse in paint and prayer.

I was no savior, just a pulse choking on truth. Sarmad's coin burned in my pocket, hot as my fading blood, my sister's ghost heavier than my journal, its pages fraying like her hospital bed's sheets. Bodh Gaya's relic auctions, Sarnath's QR codes, Kushinagar's burning corpse, Amritsar's langar, Dharamsala's poisoned peaks, the Sufi shrine's cracked dome, Rudra's ashram and market—they'd carved me to bone. My camera, a noose around my neck, caught the mob's cries: "Baba! Truth!" and "Traitor! Die!"

Rudra's enforcers hunted me, their vials glinting with poison—venom I'd tasted in the market's tea, seen in the temple's shadow. The mob, split by my video, tore at itself: half worshipped me, half craved my blood. I'd broken Rudra's mask, but they'd break my bones, like hyenas and vultures tearing Buddha's flesh.

I hid in a slum's edge, where shanties sagged under Delhi's weight. A child, eyes like ash, offered me water from a chipped cup. I hesitated—poison hid in every drop. "Baba," she whispered, "you're the one." Her mother knelt, clutching my t-shirt, murmuring prayers. Across the alley, men spat, fists clenched, their phones flashing my viral scream.

A shout erupted. The mob surged—worshippers chanting my name, detractors hurling stones. A rock grazed my temple, blood trickling like ink. I clutched my journal, camera swinging, and ran, their noose of eyes tightening. A woman tore my sleeve, screaming, "Bless us!" A man swung a stick, snarling, "Liar!" My boots pounded mud, heart a drum of dread.

I stumbled into a gutted factory, its rusted beams groaning like my hope. A shadow moved—an enforcer, vial in hand, kurta stained with Delhi's rot. "Rudra's mercy," he sneered, "drink, or we make you." The vial's liquid gleamed, sharp as death. I swung my camera, cracking his wrist, the vial shattering on the floor, its stench burning my throat.

I fled, lungs searing, to a rooftop overlooking Rudra's hub. The city pulsed below, a beast of greed. I wrote, journal trembling:

"They'll rip me like vultures, no grave, just scraps for their apps. Truth isn't a chant—it's a wound no prayer can seal."

I dreamt of my sister, her face fading, weaving my t-shirt into a noose. Hyenas tore my flesh, my camera's lens bleeding ink, my journal's pages dust in the wind. A mob chanted, half in worship, half in rage, their hands clawing my bones. I woke, choking, Sarmad's coin cutting my palm, her whisper—Truth feeds the hungry—a shard in my lungs.

Rudra's hub was close, its servers the root of his lies. Tomorrow, I'd face him or his dogs, burn his empire or bleed dry. Not for redemption. For her echo, fading in this city of claws.

The coin burned, hot as my fading blood. I'm no savior, but I'll scream until my bones shatter—before they tear me apart like vultures.

Chapter 19:

The Heart of Lies

Delhi's pulse thrashed, a beast of smog and steel, its arteries choked with greed. Rudra's server hub squatted in the city's core—a fortress of glass and wires, spinning lies into scripture. My scream, my video exposing his fraud, had splintered his empire, but the shards cut me deepest. Posters of my face—The Fire-Bearer, Savior or Traitor?—bled across the city, my name a wound in neon and dust.

I was no savior, just a scream drowning in truth. Sarmad's coin seared my pocket, hot as my fading blood, my sister's ghost heavier than my journal, its pages fraying like her hospital bed's sheets. Bodh Gaya's relic auctions, Sarnath's QR codes, Kushinagar's burning corpse, Amritsar's langar, Dharamsala's poisoned peaks, the Sufi shrine's cracked dome, Rudra's ashram, market, and servers—they'd stripped me to bone. My camera, a noose around my neck, caught the mob's cries: "Baba! Truth!" and "Traitor! Die!"

The exposure had torn them apart—half worshipped me, half hungered for my blood. Rudra's enforcers, vials glinting with poison, stalked closer, their venom in the market's tea, the temple's shadow, the factory's air. My scream had shattered Rudra's mask, but the mob's noose of eyes tightened, ready to tear me like hyenas and vultures tore Buddha's flesh.

I crept through a back alley, its walls scrawled with my name in prayers and curses. A beggar, face cracked like earth, offered me a roti, his eyes pleading.

I refused—poison hid in every bite, every breath. "Baba," he rasped, "you're the one." I shook my head, voice breaking. "I'm no saint. Just a wound."

He knelt, fingers brushing my boots. A crowd gathered, some chanting, others snarling, their phones flashing like vulture eyes. A stone struck my shoulder, blood seeping like ink. I clutched my journal, camera swinging, and pushed through, their worship and wrath a blade at my ribs.

The hub loomed, its glass doors gleaming like jaws. I slipped inside, past guards with diesel-stained kurtas, their eyes sharp as knives. Servers hummed, screens glowing with Rudra's lies—fake relics, forged verses, my t-shirt sold as Relic of the Fire-Bearer. A voice echoed—Rudra, on a balcony above, his silk robes a mockery of truth. "The Fire-Bearer seeks to burn us," he purred to a livestreaming crowd, "but truth is ours to sell."

I climbed the stairs, heart pounding, journal heavy as stone. "You're a thief!" I roared, voice raw as blood. "You cage gods in code, sell souls for clicks!"

His smile was venom, eyes glinting like coins. "Join me," he said, "or burn alone."

A guard lunged, vial in hand, its poison sharp as death. I dodged, slamming my camera into his chest, the vial shattering, its stench choking the air. The crowd below surged, phones raised, half chanting "Baba!" half screaming "Traitor!" A woman tore my t-shirt, another grabbed my journal. I yanked it back, pages ripping, blood dripping from my shoulder.

Rudra laughed, his voice a knife. "You're already theirs," he said, gesturing to the mob. "Your truth is my product."

I ran, through a maze of servers, their hum a hymn to greed. A door led to a rooftop, Delhi's smog a shroud below. I wrote, journal trembling:

"They'll tear my flesh like vultures, no grave, just scraps for their streams. Truth isn't a code—it's a wound no server can hold."

I dreamt of my sister, her face fading, stitching my t-shirt into a crown of thorns. Hyenas tore my bones, my camera's lens bleeding ink, my journal's pages ash in the wind. A mob chanted, half in worship, half in rage, their hands clawing my blood. I woke, gasping, Sarmad's coin cutting my palm, her whisper—Truth feeds the hungry—a shard in my heart.

Rudra's hub was the heart of his lies, but the mob was its teeth. Tomorrow, I'd face them—Rudra, his enforcers, the crowd—to burn it all or bleed dry. Not for salvation. For her echo, fading in this city of knives.

The coin seared, hot as my fading blood. I'm no saint, but I'll scream until my bones shatter—before they rip me apart like vultures.

Chapter 20:

The Wound That Sings

Delhi's heart roared, a beast forged of smog and steel, its veins pulsing with greed's black blood. Rudra's server hub towered in the city's core, a glass cathedral of lies, its wires weaving truth into chains. My scream—exposing his fraud, shattering his mask in a viral blaze—had set the city alight, but the flames devoured me. Posters of my face, The Fire-Bearer, Savior or Traitor?, bled across walls, my name a wound carved in neon and ash, a hymn sung by vultures.

I was no saint, no prophet, just a scream torn from truth's raw throat. Sarmad's coin seared my palm, hot as my ebbing blood, my sister's ghost heavier than my journal, its pages fraying like the shroud of her hospital bed. Bodh Gaya's relic auctions, Sarnath's QR-coded prayers, Kushinagar's burning corpse, Amritsar's langar, Dharamsala's poisoned peaks, the Sufi shrine's cracked dome, Rudra's ashram, market, and servers—they'd flayed me to bone, stripped me to a pulse of pain. My camera, a noose woven of light, caught the mob's cries: "Baba! Truth!" and "Traitor! Die!"

My exposure had split them—half crowned me savior, half craved my blood. Rudra's enforcers, their vials glinting with poison, had stalked me through alleys, temples, factories, their venom in every cup, every breath. The mob's noose of eyes tightened, their hands clawing like scavengers—not hyenas, not vultures, but humans, the cruelest beasts, who taught the wild to tear flesh for profit.

I stood in a public square before the hub, heart a drum of dread, journal heavy as stone. The crowd swelled, a sea of phones and fists, their chants a storm of worship and wrath. Rudra appeared, silk robes gleaming like a serpent's skin, his voice streaming to millions, a venomous hymn. "The Fire-Bearer seeks to burn our truth," he purred, "but we are the light."

I raised my camera, its lens a dying eye, and roared, voice jagged as lightning: "You cage truth in code, sell souls for coins! Truth is no relic—it's a wound that sings!"

The mob surged, a tide of human claws, wilder than any beast. A woman tore my t-shirt, threads ripping like veins. A man seized my journal, pages scattering like ash. I fought, blood dripping from my shoulder, but an enforcer slithered through, vial in hand. His needle pierced my neck, poison flooding me—clean as water, burning as fire, untamed as lightning no hand could hold. My knees buckled, the coin's sear my only anchor, my sister's whisper—Truth feeds the hungry—a blade in my soul.

In that fading pulse, I saw what the great ones saw in their final breath—not gods, not thrones, but the human beast, its claws sharper than any vulture's, its greed darker than any hyena's hunger. They forgave, as I did, my voice a trembling Orpheus' song: "Forgive them—they know not what they tear." But they didn't hear, their hands ripping my t-shirt to rags, shattering my camera, scattering my journal's pages like leaves in a storm. No funeral, no grave—just scavengers in human skin, fighting for relics to auction, to worship, their phones flashing like eyes of the underworld.

My body fell, a blue whale sinking into the deep, giving even in death—my t-shirt a banner for their lies, my journal a scripture for their greed, my camera a false eye for their faith. Humans, the cruelest of all, taught vultures their hunger, hyenas their claws. They tore me apart, not for truth, but for scraps to sell, as Rudra's smile fed his empire with my blood.

I wrote, hand trembling, ink bleeding into the earth:

"Truth is no app, no stream, no coin. It's a wound that sings, eternal, clean as water, wild as fire, fierce as lightning. Forgive the human beast—its claws carve the world's heart."

The coin fell, hot as my ebbing blood, into the dust. My sister's face flickered, her whisper fading. The mob tore at my flesh, merciless as wildlife, their greed a storm no nation could chain. Yet in my death, like a whale's fall, my truth fed the hungry—those unseen, those free, who'd hear my scream in the wind, a song to shake the underworld, to spark a fire no slave could quench.

I was gone, but my wound sang, a revolution unborn, a lightning unbound, true as the universe's pulse.

Chapter 21:

The Silence That Screams

Delhi's heart lay still, its smog a shroud over the square where my blood had spilled. The mob had torn me apart—hyenas in human skin, vultures with phones—my t-shirt shredded, my journal's pages scattered, my camera's lens cracked like a dead eye. No funeral, no grave, just relics auctioned in Rudra's market, my name a false messiah's crown. The city's pulse faded, leaving a silence heavier than death, a wound that sang no more.

I was gone, yet I lingered—an echo, a ghost, watching the aftermath through the dust of my pages. Sarmad's coin, hot as my ebbing blood, lay lost in the dirt, my sister's whisper—Truth feeds the hungry—a shard buried in the earth. Bodh Gaya's relic auctions, Sarnath's QR codes, Kushinagar's burning corpse, Amritsar's langar, Dharamsala's poisoned peaks, the Sufi shrine's cracked dome, Rudra's ashram, market, and servers—they'd carved me to nothing, yet the silence screamed my truth.

In the square, a boy clutched a scrap of my t-shirt, his eyes wet with tears he couldn't name. Was he weak for crying, or cold for standing there, holding a relic that meant nothing? A woman, face cracked like drought, bid for my journal's torn page, her voice trembling: "The Fire-Bearer's words—truth eternal." But they weren't mine—they were hers, my sister's, the hungry's, stolen by greed's claws. Rudra's empire thrived, his screens flashing my face, selling my death as salvation.

I saw them all—the worshippers, the scavengers, the silent. A beggar, eyes like ash, held my camera's broken frame, whispering, "Baba, why?" I wanted to answer: I forgave you, but you tore me still. But the silence held me, cold as stone, yet trembling like a child's sob. Death was the universal truth, inevitable as the stars, yet it broke me—not my death, but theirs, the hungry left unfed, the truth left unsung.

In the market, they fought over my relics—t-shirt rags, journal scraps, camera shards—like vultures over a whale's fall. My death fed them, not with truth, but with lies they could sell. A girl, no older than my sister once was, clutched a page, reading: "Truth is a wound that sings, eternal, clean as water, wild as fire, fierce as lightning." Her tears fell, soft as rain, and I wondered: was she weak for crying, or strong for feeling the wound? I'd seen horrors—bodies piled in shadows, screams swallowed by greed—yet never wept. But for a small bird, wings still, I'd sobbed like a child, my heart a wound no coldness could seal.

The silence grew, a scream without sound. Was it waste, my death? I'd screamed for truth, exposed Rudra's lies, but they crowned me a messiah I wasn't. The boy's tears, the girl's trembling hands—they held my truth, not Rudra's apps. My death was no waste if one heart heard, one soul felt the wound. Like a whale sinking, I fed the unseen, the free, those who'd carry my scream in their bones.

A wind stirred, scattering my journal's ashes. The coin gleamed in the dust, untouched. The silence screamed, not for me, but for them—the human beast, tearing itself apart, yet yearning for the truth it buried. I was no saint, but my wound sang, a song to shake the earth, to free the chained, to burn the lies to ash.

The boy wiped his eyes, the girl clutched the page, and the silence held them, fragile as a bird's wing, fierce as a revolution unborn.

Chapter 22:

The Truth We Killed

Delhi's heart lay silent, a grave of smog and steel, its pulse choked by greed's black ash. The square where I fell—torn by human claws, my t-shirt shredded, my journal's pages scattered, my camera's lens a dead eye—now pulsed with a new lie. They called me The Fire-Bearer, a messiah I never was, their phones flashing my relics on Rudra's screens, auctioned for coins, worshipped for nothing. My death, my scream for truth, was a wound they refused to feel.

I lingered, not as flesh but as echo, a ghost in the dust where Sarmad's coin lay, still hot as my ebbing blood. My sister's whisper—Truth feeds the hungry—faded into the earth, unheeded. Bodh Gaya's relic auctions, Sarnath's QR codes, Kushinagar's burning corpse, Amritsar's langar, Dharamsala's poisoned peaks, the Sufi shrine's cracked dome, Rudra's ashram, market, and servers—they'd flayed me to nothing, yet the truth I died for was buried in their greed.

In the market, a boy held my t-shirt's rag, now a "relic" sold for thousands, his eyes dry, cold as stone. Was he weak for not crying, or strong for swallowing the lie? A girl, clutching my journal's torn page, read my words aloud: "Truth is a wound that sings, eternal, clean as water, wild as fire, fierce as lightning." Her voice trembled, but the crowd drowned her, chanting my name as if I were their god. They didn't hear—humanity was the path, not babas, not rituals, not Rudra's apps. I'd sought myself, sought the light, screamed it was in us, not in coins or relics. But they killed me for it, their claws sharper than any vulture's, their greed darker than any hyena's hunger.

The silence of my death was a scream they ignored. They crowned me a savior, but my truth was dead, and they had killed it. I saw it now, as the great ones saw: humanity, the highest mind on this earth, is the fool that slays its own. They tore me apart, not for enlightenment, but for scraps to sell, to worship. My death was no whale's fall, feeding the hungry—it was a waste, a wound they'd never feel.

A wind stirred, scattering my journal's ashes. The boy dropped the t-shirt, the girl let the page fall, and Rudra's empire thrived, his screens flashing my face as a product. The truth I died for—humanity's heart, raw and unadorned—was too bitter to digest. Those who speak it die, by the crowd's paws or the masters' poison. I forgave them, but they didn't care, their hands too busy clawing relics to hear my song.

And yet, in the unseen, a spark flickered—a soul, maybe one, heard my scream. My truth, buried in the earth, waited like a seed for a revolution unborn. But the weight of their blindness crushed me, a silence louder than death.

"Truth is dead, and we have killed it." —Guru Kripa Deep Singh

"The human beast, crowned with mind, is the fool that tears its own heart." —Guru Kripa Deep Singh

"We slay the light-bearers, then worship their bones—our greed is our god." —Guru Kripa Deep Singh

"Enlightenment is no relic, no app—it's the wound we fear to feel." —Guru Kripa Deep Singh

"I died for truth, but you crowned my corpse—humanity is the grave of its own soul." —Guru Kripa Deep Singh

"Enlightenment demands sacrifice without limit. Its price can be your very life—whether you surrender it willingly or it is taken from you. When you draw near to the divine, humanity may turn against you, forcing you toward the ultimate offering. Some walk to death; others are driven there by poison, by mobs, or by the hands of those who cannot bear the light." —Guru Kripa Deep Singh

The coin lay in the dust, untouched. My sister's face flickered, then faded. The silence screamed, a wound eternal, too raw for their hearts, too true for their eyes. They'd fear to face it again, to read my ashes, to know they killed the truth they could never digest. My scream lingered, a song for the unseen, a fire no slave could chain, a lightning no nation could hold.